My Little Pony The Movie

pi kids® Phoenix International Publications, Inc.

Chicago • London • New York • Hamburg • Mexico City • Paris • Sydney

Equestria's first-ever Friendship Festival is about to begin! As princess in charge, Twilight Sparkle has so much to do. Luckily, she has amazing friends who are more than happy to help. Pinkie Pie's confetti cake cannon still needs a little work, but everypony is pitching in!

Look for these friendly finds around the fairground:

FREE to Friends

sign

this cloud

Angel Bunny

gemstone

candle

Discord balloon

What's this? Tempest Shadow has landed! She demands all of the princesses' magic… and is certainly a bit stony when she is denied. Tempest's leader, the Storm King, expects Equestria's total surrender. His Storm Creatures are ready to make sure he gets it!

The battle has begun! Can you spot these invaders in the attackers' ranks?

Grubber

these Storm Creatures

Only Twilight Sparkle and her friends have managed to escape, with Princess Celestia's plea to "seek help from the Queen of the Hippo..." ringing in their ears. Finding the Hippos won't be easy. Perhaps the ponies can bargain for directions in Klugetown, a place where everything has its price.

The road to Klugetown has been long and hard. Can you find these landmarks along the way?

road sign

animal skull

this footprint

petroglyph

this cactus

sunglasses

Klugetown doesn't welcome strangers, but the ponies have made a feline friend named Capper. Or have they? Capper wants to move up in the world, and selling his new pals would finance the life he'd like to lead. It looks like Twilight Sparkle and her friends have walked into even more trouble!

Capper's possessions are tattered, but treasured. Look around for these beloved belongings:

doily

record

plant

teacups

fan

atlas

The ponies are on the run again! They try hitching a ride aboard an airship manned by parrot pirates, but Tempest's ship-snagging harpoon forces an emergency bailout. The ponies are plunging to the ground, along with the airship's cargo!

Look out below! Spot this falling flotsam:

mirror

flour sack

this crate

poster

this crate

bushel of apples

Luckily, the travelers land in the "Hippo" homeland, where they discover that they're really looking for Hippo*griffs*, part pony and part eagle. With her Pearl of Transformation, the Hippogriffs' Queen Novo has changed all her subjects into Seaponies to protect them from the Storm King. She transforms her pony guests too!

While Twilight Sparkle considers "borrowing" the power of the Pearl, look around for these throne room things:

Spike

this jellyfish

this coral

royal crown

Pearl

Jamal

When the Mane Six resurface as ponies again, Twilight Sparkle is captured by Tempest and taken to Canterlot. The Storm King summons a tornado to whirl Twilight Sparkle's rescuers away, but he gets caught in it himself when his magic goes awry. Will the ponies retrieve the king's staff of power before he does?

The staff's wild magic is destroying everything! Can you spot this whirlwind wreckage?

helmet

this cupcake

Spike

rope

banner

Shelly

The Storm King has been vanquished! Now Equestria is ready to have some fun. All of the ponies' new friends, including Tempest, are joining the victory party, too. After all, there's no better place to celebrate friendship (and eat cake!) than the Friendship Festival!

Can you find all of these party particulars?

Capper's hat

Twilight Sparkle's crown

Spike's sunglasses

this partygoer

Grubber's cake

pirate's hook

Skystar's necklace

The ponies don't know it yet, but they're about to begin an alarming adventure! Flip back to the Friendship Festival to find these tokens of things to come:

orb

staff

map

beetle

seashell

hippo

Tempest is preparing Canterlot for the arrival of the Storm King. Inch back to the invasion to look for these things that prove his power:

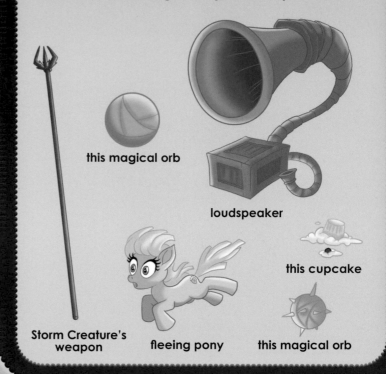

this magical orb

loudspeaker

this cupcake

Storm Creature's weapon

fleeing pony

this magical orb

Tempest isn't the only one interested in the wanderers' whereabouts. Dash back to the desert to find these inhabitants who are watching their every step:

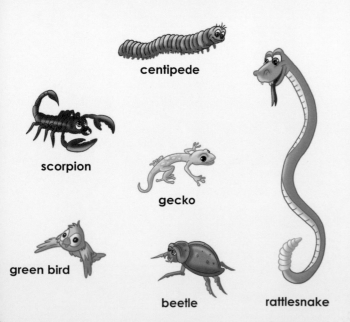

centipede

scorpion

gecko

green bird

beetle

rattlesnake

Capper's means may be meager, but he sure has a lot of stuff! Hustle back to his home to find more household goods:

statuette

portrait

hat

wine glass

clock

sweater

candle

The airship's crew of scoundrels were pirates once…and they'll "get awesome" again! Slip back to the ship to spot these reminders of the parrots' past:

skull and crossbones sign

treasure map

gold doubloons

pirate flag

pirate hat

sword

Princess Skystar is thrilled to have some new friends who aren't crustaceans! Caper back to Queen Novo's court to spot these shelly specimens:

Sheldon

Shelly

these seashells

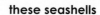

Friendship has bound Twilight and her pals into an unstoppable force. Turn back to the tornado to find a symbol of each pony in the chain:

Twilight Sparkle

Rainbow Dash

Pinkie Pie

Applejack

Rarity

Fluttershy

Tempest has a little secret. Her real name is… wait for it…Fizzlepop Berrytwist! Look back through each spread in the book to find the letters that spell F - I - Z - Z - L - E - P - O - P.

That is the most awesome name *ever!*